DO YOU ENJOY BEING FRIGHTENED?

WOULD YOU RATHER HAVE
NIGHTMARES
INSTEAD OF SWEET DREAMS?

ARE YOU HAPPY ONLY WHEN
SHAKING WITH FEAR?

CONGRATULATIONS!!!!

YOU'VE MADE A WISE CHOICE.

THIS BOOK IS THE DOORWAY
TO ALL THAT MAY FRIGHTEN YOU.

GET READY FOR

COLD, CLAMMY SHIVERS
RUNNING UP AND DOWN YOUR SPINE!

NOW, OPEN THE DOOR~
IF YOU DARE!

Shivers®

NIGHT OF
THE GOAT BOY

M. D. Spenser

Chapter One

It was not a very scary face.

Weird, yes. Ugly, definitely. But not really scary at all.

The eyeballs seemed to be jutting out a little bit more than usual. The nostrils were pretty big, there was no doubt. The teeth were bared in a snarl, and since some of them were missing, that did look a little gross.

From out of that mouth came a rasping growl — "R-r-r-r-r-r-r" — that sounded like a six-year-old kid imitating a grizzly bear.

It sounded that way because that's exactly what it was: a six-year-old kid imitating a grizzly bear. In the back seat of a minivan.

Nope, not too scary at all.

"Oh wow, I'm terrified," Nathaniel told his six-year-old sister, Amanda. She had stuck her fingertips under her eyelids and pulled them down, pulled her nostrils up and showed off her missing teeth.

"Nathaniel, you were supposed to be afraid," she whined. She loved teasing her eleven-year-old brother whenever she could, whether it meant making faces at him or sneaking into his room when he was gone.

Nathaniel, like most older brothers, put up with her, loved her — and found her annoying. Today was not a day when he had the time or inclination to pay attention to her.

"How much longer?" he asked his parents, who sat in the front of the van as it hurtled along the highway.

"About another hour," his dad said, keeping his eyes on the road.

Nathaniel felt so excited he could hardly keep still. He was on his way to Camp Spotlight, a special summer camp for youngsters interested in drama.

Ever since he could remember, Nathaniel had liked plays. He liked acting in them, and he liked writing them on his family's computer at home.

That made him different from a lot of other eleven-year-old boys. But in other ways he was typical. When he and his friends got together, they'd play basketball and football and baseball.

It seemed as if his slender, limber body had been made for sports. He was medium height for his age, and while eleven-year-old boys rarely had very much muscle, he was starting to develop some in his upper arms.

On the basketball court, he would practically fly with the ball, his light brown hair flopping as he ran, his gray eyes locked on the basket.

As much as he liked sports, Nathaniel loved plays even more. He didn't know where this love had come from, because neither of his parents had ever been involved in drama.

His mom was a kindergarten teacher. His dad wrote comic books for a living, which most of his friends thought was either a really strange thing for a father to do, or a really cool thing, or both.

Sometimes, when the weather was bad and he

and his friends were just hanging around the house, Nathaniel would print one of the plays he had written on his computer. He'd give copies to his friends and cast them and have them perform.

The first time he had done this, his friends had thought it was a dopey idea, but they were bored and went along with it. To their surprise they had found they liked it.

It wasn't as much fun as playing baseball, but it was better than playing the same video game for the one millionth time.

So when Nathaniel had read about Camp Spotlight, for kids interested in drama, he had begged and begged his parents to let him go. They had seemed reluctant at first, his mom especially.

That was when he first felt that something just wasn't right.

His parents had enough money for him to go to the camp. They knew how much he loved acting in plays. Yet they kept making excuses and delaying a decision. Nathaniel kept bugging them, though, until, finally, they had agreed to let him go.

The night they told him they would allow him to go to camp, they told him something strange.

"Your dad and I met at Camp Spotlight, thirty years ago," his mother said. "We didn't really fall in love then, because we were eleven, just like you are. But we came back the next year, and the next, and pretty soon we got to be friends, and so on."

Nathaniel was puzzled. His parents had gone to Camp Spotlight. But he thought they had never been interested in plays. At least that's what they had always told him.

So why all of a sudden were they telling him they had gone to Camp Spotlight years ago?

He was tempted to ask them that question, but he was too anxious to keep the talk focused on him.

"Well, I kind of got the feeling you weren't real wild about me going," he told them.

His mother looked down at her lap. His father looked off to one side.

"Really?" his father said, in a strange tone of voice. "Whatever makes you say that, son?"

"You just kept avoiding it every time I would

bring it up," Nathaniel said.

His parents glanced at each other quickly, then looked away.

"Well, we decided it was OK for you to go," his mother said brightly. "And that's what you wanted, wasn't it?"

Yes, that was what he wanted. But he also wanted to know why his parents were nervous.

He had been away to camp before, even though that was when he was a Boy Scout and his dad was a scoutmaster, and they had gone together. But, hey, he was eleven years old, and it wasn't like he was asking to go live by himself in California and be a surfer or something.

It was just a summer camp. What could make his parents nervous about a summer camp?

Was there, he wondered, something they weren't telling him?

Chapter Two

Nathaniel looked out the window as the countryside flew by.

He liked living in the suburbs near shopping malls and movie theaters and his school, and he had never been out in the country very much.

It just seemed so huge; there was so much of it.

A field ran beside the highway, and beyond the field stood some woods. The woods seemed dark and thick. It looked as if they went on forever.

Nathaniel's mind drifted.

He found himself remembering something weird from a week ago. He had been in bed asleep and had suddenly woken up, thirsty. The glass of water he usually kept by his bedside was empty, so he had picked it up and gone downstairs to the kitchen to refill it.

He paused outside his parents' bedroom door. Their light was on and the door was cracked. He could hear them talking — about him and Camp Spotlight.

"But what if it's gotten worse?" his mom asked his dad.

What if *what's* gotten worse, Nathaniel wondered. He knew he shouldn't be eavesdropping on a private conversation between his parents, but now he had to know what they were talking about.

What if *what* had gotten worse?

"Come on, hon," his dad said to his mom. "It's going to be fine. We survived, didn't we?"

" I know we did," his mom said. "I'm just . . . I don't know. I just don't know if he's ready yet."

Nathaniel felt his heart pounding beneath his pajamas as he listened.

"Maybe we should tell him," his mom said.

"I don't think that would be fair to the other kids," his dad replied. "Look, it's just a part of the Camp Spotlight experience. It's been going on for

8

years. Nathaniel really wants to go there, and he's eleven years old. What's the worst that can happen?"

Nathaniel didn't know what the worst that could happen was, but he wanted to know. He found this whole conversation unsettling.

"All right," he heard his mother say. "I'll go along. It was OK for us, wasn't it?"

"Sure it was," his dad said. "He'll be fine."

*   *   *

"Hey, *Nathaniel!*"

"Huh? What?" He had been lost deep inside this disturbing memory.

"Come on, Nathaniel, play a game with me!"

It was his kid sister Amanda again. Nathaniel wanted to ask his parents what they had been talking about that night, but Amanda kept insisting on a game.

Nathaniel's dad spoke up from the front seat.

"No time for a game, guys," he said. "This is our exit coming right up. After that, it's only a couple of miles to camp."

9

Only a couple of miles! Nathaniel started squirming.

He quickly forgot all about the conversation he had overheard between his parents and started gazing out the window. He stared with all his might, as if the harder he looked the sooner he would see the camp.

After a few minutes, his dad turned the minivan onto a gravel road. A huge wooden sign overhead read: WELCOME TO CAMP SPOT-LIGHT.

He was finally here!

His dad pulled the van into a parking lot alongside several other cars and vans. Other kids were piling out and looking around with excitement.

Nobody knew anybody else yet, so hardly any of the kids were talking to each other.

Moms and dads pulled duffel bags, suitcases and trunks out of the cars. Everything seemed to be labeled with kids' names and addresses.

Nathaniel glanced at some of the tags, and noticed a few from his town, a few from a nearby city, and a lot from places around the state he had never been to.

There was a lot do during the next few minutes.

He had to register and fill out a health form, which his parents helped him with. His dad wrote a check while his mom filled out some other forms.

A nurse checked him for head lice, which was pretty embarrassing, since she had to poke all through his hair. But he had seen the kids before him go through this and he knew the kids after him would have to do the same.

He was assigned to Tent Number Five, wherever that was. A teenage girl with a nametag that read "Molly" pointed down a long trail and told him that he'd find his tent at the end of the trail.

"Well, son," his dad said. "I guess this is where we say good-bye. Have a great two weeks. You'll be fine."

"I slipped a few candy bars into your suitcase," his mom said. "As I remember, the food here isn't all that great."

"Thanks, Mom," Nathaniel said.

There was an awkward pause.

"Oh, honey, do have fun — and whatever happens, don't worry," his mom said. She hugged him tight. As if *she* was worried.

When his mom released him, his dad stepped over and hugged him even tighter.

"Mom, Dad, I . . . "

Nathaniel was about to ask them about the conversation he had overheard that night while standing in the hall. He wanted to ask why they had been reluctant to let him go, and why they had been so nervous on the car trip coming up here.

But he was interrupted.

"Attention all campers!" the voice boomed, nasal and amplified. "Please report to your tents immediately!"

A teenage boy with a nametag that read "Matthew" was hollering through a megaphone to make himself heard. Nathaniel didn't get to finish his question.

He told his parents good-bye, that he loved them, then turned to walk down the trail to his tent.

Amanda called, "Bye, Nathaniel." Then, as he looked over his shoulder, his parents took Amanda by the hand and got back into the minivan. As he walked down the trail toward Tent Number Five, the van backed out of the parking lot and drove away.

For the first time in his life, Nathaniel was separated from his parents and his little sister. And in a place he had never been to before.

He felt excited, tingly — and maybe just a little bit scared.

Chapter Three

When Nathaniel reached Tent Number Five, he saw that all three of his tent-mates were already there and unpacking.

"Hey, dude," said a short boy with glasses. "My name's Jacques. How ya doin'?"

"Hi, I'm Nathaniel."

"This is Chris," Jacques said, pointing to a suntanned boy wearing a baseball cap backwards on his head. Chris waved, and Nathaniel waved back.

"And I'm Brian," said the third boy, who had dark bangs that flopped almost into his eyes.

"This your first time?" asked Brian.

"Yeah," said Nathaniel.

"Ours, too," said Jacques. "We were all just talking about it. Did any of your friends think it was weird that you were going to a drama camp?"

"No," Nathaniel answered. "Uh-uh."

"*My* friends did, and so did Chris's," said Jacques. "They thought it was kind of a sissy thing. They all wanted to go to sports camps or adventure camps or running camps or rock-climbing camps or something. So I said, fine, whatever."

Nathaniel could tell Jacques was going to be a real talker.

"Yeah, whatever," Nathaniel said. "My friends were cool. It was my parents who were freaky."

"Freaky? How?" asked Brian.

Even though he had just met them, Nathaniel found himself telling his three tent-mates how he had overheard his parent's conversation, and how it had worried him.

When he finished, nobody said anything.

Finally, Jacques broke the silence.

"Man, your parents are weird," he said.

"Yeah, but they've been here themselves," Nathaniel said. "So maybe they know something we don't."

"Whatever," Jacques said.

There were four cots in the tent, and three of them had stuff on them already. Nathaniel started unpacking. He unrolled his sleeping bag and laid it on top of the one unoccupied cot the way the other boys had. He opened his suitcase, pulled out his pillow, closed the case full of clothes and stuffed it under the cot.

Jacques, Chris and Brian were talking.

"So what are we gonna do here?" Brian asked.

"We're gonna rehearse and perform a play," Chris replied.

"Sounds cool," Brian said. "So long as I get to be the star."

"Yeah, you wish," Jacques said. "There's gonna be one star at Camp Spotlight, and that's the guy who's talking right now. Namely me."

"Well, you're nearly always the guy talking though, aren't you?" shot back Chris.

"Ooh, burn," said Brian. He licked his finger and touched it to Jacques's forehead and made a s-s-s-s-s-s sizzling sound.

"Outta my face," said Jacques, swiping at

Brian's hand.

Nathaniel smiled. These guys were gonna be fun.

"Goooooood afternoon, Tent Five!" a voice boomed.

A man had poked his head in the open flap of the tent. He was mostly bald, with a fringe of black curly hair around the edges of his head. He wore thick glasses that made his eyes look weird, like fish eyes.

As he stepped into the tent, Nathaniel saw that the man was wearing a red-and-white polka-dot shirt, plaid shorts, black socks and heavy sandals. He was carrying a clipboard.

Nathaniel thought the guy ought to be in a museum. You know, where they had a figure for Neanderthal Man, and Cro-Magnon Man, and Modern Man.

This guy, whoever he was, would be perfect as Dweeb Man.

"My name is Mr. Dingle," Dweeb Man said, "and I'm the camp director here at Camp Spotlight. You four are all first-timers, so I wanted to extend to each of you an extra, extra, special welcome."

The four boys, realizing they were in the presence of a grownup who was the opposite of everything they would ever want to be, looked at the floor and shuffled their feet.

"Hey."

"Yeah."

"Whatever."

They all looked at the floor, not wanting to make eye contact with Dweeb Man.

"So, you're all unpacked?" Mr. Dingle said brightly. "Very, very good. Excellent. Excellent! Will you all please join us for roll call and orientation?"

"Yeah."

"Whatever."

The boys scuffed their sneakered toes against the wooden planks on the floor of their tent. Even Jacques, Mr. Talkative, had nothing to say.

"Wonderful, wonderful," said Mr. Dingle, who seemed to enjoy repeating everything he said. "See you in the clearing in five minutes. Ta ta!"

After he left, Nathaniel looked at Jacques.

Chris looked at Brian. All four boys burst out laughing.

"Ta ta!" mimicked Jacques.

"Wonderful, wonderful," echoed Nathaniel.

They laughed again, and slapped palms, and laughed some more. Then they walked to the clearing for roll call.

*   *   *

When they got there, the clearing was full of campers. About half were boys and half were girls.

Nathaniel was just starting to get interested in girls.

He had grown out of the stage of thinking girls were yucky and had cooties and were to be avoided at all costs. But he hadn't really grown into the next stage yet, where he actually *liked* them. So he was kind of in between.

But he definitely noticed when there was a pretty one — and he saw a pretty one now, standing to one side of the clearing talking with two other girls.

She had long red hair and the longest eyelashes Nathaniel had ever seen.

"OK, OK, campers, listen up!" boomed Mr. Dingle.

He was standing on a tree stump, shouting to be heard over the noise of forty kids aged ten, eleven and twelve, all of whom were talking at once.

"Welcome to Camp Spotlight!" Mr. Dingle yelled. "You're going to have the best two weeks of your young lives here, two weeks you will remember for the rest of your lives. First I need to take roll. When I call your name, please say 'Here.'

"Mary!"

"Here," said a girl.

"Rebecca."

"Here," said another.

"Anthony."

"Yo!" said a tall boy. Several kids giggled.

"Vanessa."

"That's me!"

"Jillian!"

"Here," said the red-headed girl.

Jillian, Nathaniel thought. So that's her name.

Chapter Four

Mr. Dingle finished the roll call.

"This year," he boomed, "Camp Spotlight is going to perform the musical 'You're a Good Man, Charlie Brown.' There will not be on-stage parts for every single camper. We will hold auditions starting tomorrow."

Several of the campers exchanged glances.

"Those of you who are not chosen for singing parts will still be important to the production," Mr. Dingle continued. "You will make the sets, run the lights and do all the things that are so necessary for the show to go on.

"I know you all must be hungry and it's close to dinner time, so why don't we all head over to the mess hall and have dinner? Then, tonight, we'll have one of our great Camp Spotlight traditions — a campfire and ghost stories."

The campers all filed over to the mess hall, which was a large wooden building on one side of the clearing. Nathaniel continued to hang out with his new buddies, Jacques, Chris and Brian.

They grabbed a tray and went through the dinner line. They were served by the camp's teenage counselors, all of whom wore identical white T-shirts with the words "Camp Spotlight" printed across them, and had nametags pinned to the shirts.

A girl whose tag read Megan dipped a serving spoon into a pan and plopped a piece of gravy-covered meat onto Nathaniel's plate. It made a splatting sound when it hit.

"Yum!" said Nathaniel sarcastically. Chris and Brian laughed.

"Mystery meat, just like at the school cafeteria," said Jacques. "In case we're homesick, I guess."

Nathaniel thought back to what his mother had said about the food not being very good at Camp Spotlight. Boy, was he ever glad he had a stash of candy bars waiting for him back at the tent!

Most of the campers sat with their tent-mates. Since they all came from different parts of the state, their tent-mates were the only kids most campers knew so far.

Probably all of them are away from home for the first time, like me, Nathaniel thought. The guys in my tent aren't the same as my friends back home, but at least I know them a little bit. It's good to know *someone*, at least a little bit.

The meat didn't taste all that bad. Or maybe it just tasted good compared to the mixed vegetables, which had obviously come out of a can — and probably a very old can at that.

Still, Nathaniel and his friends were hungry. They complained about the food and made jokes about it. But they ate it.

When the campers left the mess hall, it was twilight. Darkness was coming to Camp Spotlight.

Nathaniel noticed several of the teenage counselors piling logs and branches into a circle. They dragged wooden benches out of a building that had a sign on the front that read: "Camp Spotlight Performance Hall."

Some counselors arranged the benches in a circle around the growing pile of wood, while others laid the logs and branches on the pile in a criss-cross pattern.

Nathaniel figured the counselors were probably former campers like himself, older kids with a love of theater who had come here as eleven- and twelve-year-olds and now were back working here.

The campers milled about, talking and telling little stories. Hardly any of them were shy. After all, they had all come here because they loved performing. They told jokes, and laughter rang out through the clearing.

Nathaniel felt good about being at Camp Spotlight.

He saw a counselor light the campfire. A tiny flame buried under the pile of logs struggled and flickered, but then it grew taller and licked the upper logs in the pile. Soon it looked almost like a living thing, snapping and popping and dancing in the cool evening air.

Darkness had come quickly, as it does in the country. No other lights lit the area, not even the glow of a distant city. It was a cloudy night, so there were no stars or moon.

It was very dark.

The campers moved toward the wooden benches around the campfire, seeking its warmth and its light.

Mr. Dingle appeared.

"OK, wonderful, wonderful, very good," he said. Even though the night had gotten chilly, Mr. Dingle was still dressed in shorts and sandals.

"Anybody up for a ghost story?" he asked.

The kids all nodded and murmured, "Yeah, sure."

It turned out to be, Nathaniel thought, the lamest ghost story he had ever heard. Mr. Dingle obviously did not want to scare the kids, and his story was about some girl's boyfriend who died and came back to haunt her.

There wasn't any point to the story, Nathaniel thought. I could do better than that.

Finally, Mr. Dingle ended his story. Not a single camper looked the least bit afraid. Some rolled their eyes. A few of the boys squirmed restlessly.

"I'm afraid I have to go take care of some paperwork now," Mr. Dingle said. "Austin, Andrew, will you take over for me?"

Two teenage boys stepped forward. Only they didn't look like boys. They looked more like men.

Each stood about six feet tall, and their muscled arms looked as if they had spent some time working out in a gym. Both had obviously shaved for several years.

Nathaniel guessed they were seventeen or eighteen years old. For a kid of eleven, they might as well have been thirty.

"Sure thing, Mr. D," said the counselor whose nametag read Andrew.

"Take your time, Mr. D," said the other, who had to be Austin. "We'll entertain the kiddies for you."

There was something in Austin's voice that Nathaniel didn't like. It sounded as if he looked down on the campers he was theoretically there to help.

Austin waited until Mr. Dingle was no longer in sight.

"OK, ya little babies, listen up," he said. He sounded angry. "This ain't no Dingle story. This is the real thing. Anybody here nervous about coming to this camp?"

Nathaniel thought it would be foolish to raise his hand. He didn't like Austin, and thought that, if he raised his hand, he would just be asking to be picked on.

Austin sounded like a bully, the kind of guy who got his jollies humiliating kids who were younger or weaker than he was.

"Well, maybe some of you were nervous," Austin continued. "Maybe you had reason to be. And I'm the guy who's going to tell you why. The story you are about to hear is true. No names have been changed to protect the innocent. Because in this story, no one is innocent.

"This is the story of the Goat Boy."

Chapter Five

As the campers sat around the flickering glow of the campfire, Austin told the story of the Goat Boy.

"This happened about thirty years ago, right here at Camp Spotlight," he said.

Nathaniel's ears pricked up. Thirty years ago? That was when his parents had said they first met at Camp Spotlight.

Was there a connection between his parents and the Goat Boy? Was this a true story, or just something Austin had made up to scare the campers?

"Look over there at those woods," Austin commanded, pointing to his right. Every single camper's head turned to look where he was pointing.

They could see the woods, but not very well. The night was so dark, and the woods were just a place where it got even darker.

"Those woods go on for about a mile," Austin said. "On the other side of the woods, there used to be a farm. This old guy lived there, and he raised goats and chickens for a living.

"The old guy had a teenage son named Kenny. It was Kenny's job to tend the goats. Now, goats are awful, ugly, smelly creatures. They eat just about anything, so they've got the worst breath you can imagine. They're really dirty.

"And they're mean. They're nasty. They're the meanest, nastiest animals God put on this earth. If you were to try and feed a goat with your bare hand, it would bite you just for the sheer joy of doing it.

"And teeth? You can't imagine how strong their teeth are. Hey, they eat tin cans and stuff. They have to be strong. So you get a goat biting your hand, you've got problems. Like maybe losing your whole hand."

Not one camper made a sound. This didn't sound like a ghost story. This sounded like something else, something more real, something very uncomfortable.

Nathaniel gazed into the fire. The pattern of the flames seemed to hypnotize him. He heard Austin's voice, as if from a distance, telling the story of the Goat Boy.

"Kenny hated tending the goats," Austin said. "What Kenny really wanted was to be an actor. That's something you little twerps can probably identify with, right? Wanting to be an actor? Well, you're lucky. Your parents pay for you to come to Camp Spotlight.

"But Kenny's father would not. He wanted Kenny to grow up to be a goat farmer like he was, and not waste his time on something silly like acting. So he refused to send Kenny to Camp Spotlight, even though Kenny could have just walked here.

"Eventually, that's what Kenny started doing. When he got to be about eleven years old, he would sometimes take off and cut through the woods. He'd stand at the edge of the woods and watch the campers at Camp Spotlight playing and having fun.

"And he was so jealous. Oh, he was jealous.

"But he smelled bad. Hey, the kid hung out with goats all day, right? So every time he appeared at the edge of the woods, the campers here smelled him.

"Kids can be so cruel, can't they? They can tease and make fun of people, and if they don't like someone they can make his or her life miserable. That's what the kids at Camp Spotlight did.

"Whenever Kenny would appear, they'd laugh at him. They nicknamed him the Goat Boy. They'd imitate the sound a goat makes: Meh-heh-heh-heh. And they'd laugh some more.

"This went on for most of the summer. Kenny would watch, and the kids would taunt him.

"An anger started building inside Kenny. It started small, but it grew and grew. He felt angry at his father, angry at his goats, angry at the spoiled kids who got to go to camp while he couldn't.

"Finally he couldn't take it anymore," Austin said. "Something just snapped inside poor Kenny. He had to take revenge."

Austin paused. The campers scooted closer to each other on the benches. Whether or not you knew the person sitting next to you, it felt good to be in a group, and not to feel like your neighbor was too far away.

This is really creeping me out, Nathaniel thought. Even though he had laughed at Mr. Dingle's dumb, unscary story, he wished Dingle would come back from whatever paperwork he was doing.

He wished Dingle would come back and say, "That's enough, Austin. You're scaring these poor kids half to death. The Goat Boy. What nonsense!"

But Mr. Dingle didn't come back. And Austin went on with his story.

Nathaniel felt as if it were no longer the present. Austin was such a good story-teller that it seemed like it was really thirty years in the past, and this group of campers had teased Kenny, the Goat Boy.

The light of the campfire flickered across Austin's face. Nathaniel could tell the counselor was enjoying telling such a weird story to the kids.

"One night, well after midnight," Austin continued, "everyone in the camp was asleep. Kenny snuck through the woods and into the camp. The counselors had built a campfire that night, just like the one we have here. They had put it out, but some embers still glowed at the bottom.

"Kenny poked around in the campfire till he found a glowing ember. He blew on it, and the extra oxygen made the ember glow hotter. He touched some leaves to it to give it something to burn, and soon he had a burning stick in his hand.

"He walked to one of the tents with the burning stick in his hand. The anger burned inside of him, too.

"He paused for a minute. Not that he was having second thoughts about what he was going to do. He was enjoying the moment.

"Then he touched the burning stick to the cloth tent. And the tent, full of campers like yourselves, burst into flame!"

Chapter Six

The campers held their breath.

They were already nervous about their first night in these tents, and now they were listening to a story about one of the tents being on fire!

"Luckily, the boys inside the tent woke up," Austin said. "They rushed out just as the flames consumed the tent. They were not hurt, but you can imagine how scared they were.

"The camp director at the time called the police, who came and investigated. But no one saw Kenny set the tent on fire and there was no proof. Everybody believed he had done it, but he couldn't be arrested without proof.

"Then it came time for the campers' parents to come pick them up. Of course, the first thing everybody did was talk about Kenny and the fire and the

35

police and all that. The parents were very upset.

"And one parent was the most upset of all. He was the father of one of the boys in the tent that burned. And he was a magician who called himself Muldaur the Magnificent.

"He did magic shows at state fairs and stuff like that. He would saw a lady in half, or pull a rabbit out of the hat, or take a purse from a lady in the crowd and turn it into a live chicken and then turn it back into her purse.

"Fun stuff. And everybody would clap.

"But what the crowd didn't know — and what even his own family didn't know — was that Muldaur the Magnificent could do real magic.

"We all believe in magic when we're little. Then we get older, and we learn that real magic doesn't exist. But it *does*. It always has, from the beginning of time. Certain people have the power. Sometimes they use it for good. Sometimes they use it for evil.

"And sometimes they use it for revenge."

The campers sat spellbound in the flickering

light, all eyes turned on Austin.

"When Muldaur the Magnificent heard that his son had almost been burned alive by Kenny, his rage knew no bounds," Austin said. "He was insane with anger. He drove his son home, hardly speaking a word.

"Then Muldaur turned right around and drove back to Camp Spotlight. Only he didn't drive into the camp. He took the exit before the camp exit, and turned off onto another road — the road that led to Kenny's father's farm.

"Kenny was asleep in his bed. It was a dark, starless, moonless night, just like tonight. Muldaur looked through the window at the sleeping boy. He muttered a spell under his breath. The spell was that Kenny would forever be half-human, and half-goat.

"A real, living Goat Boy.

"To this very day," Austin said, peering through the orange firelight at the campers, the Goat Boy haunts the woods around Camp Spotlight. But now he has grown into a Goat Man. He has the head of a goat and the body of a human.

"He has the same awful smell goats have. He makes an awful goatish cry that can chill your blood.

Austin's voice dropped to a whisper. Nathaniel and the other campers leaned toward him, not wanting to miss a word.

"And he eats anything. And everything."

Austin paused. Something rustled in the woods behind him. Every camper looked at the woods, trying to see what had made the noise.

An eerie, piercing sound came out of the woods, like the cry of something in pain and angry at the same time.

"Meh-heh-heh! Meh-heh-heh!"

"Oh, my gosh!" Austin shouted.

<u>Chapter Seven</u>

The camp erupted into panic.

The trees rustled and swayed, as if something were crashing through them, running straight for the campfire.

Kids jumped from their benches, their eyes wild with terror. Screams and cries echoed through the night. Benches fell over backwards as kids jumped from them. In the confusion, some kids ran into each other.

A figure leaped from the woods.

It was Andrew, the other teenage counselor.

"Ha! Ha!" he laughed at the frightened campers. "Boy you ought to see the looks on your faces!"

He walked over to Austin. The two bullies exchanged high fives.

The roaring fire, the sound of Austin's voice,

and the strange story had hypnotized everyone. Nobody had seen Andrew sneak away from the group and enter the woods, waiting for the right moment in Austin's story to jump out and scare the living daylights out of the campers.

"Whew," Nathaniel said. He blew out a big breath, trying to relax himself. He turned to Jacques, who was standing next to him.

Jacques was pale, as if he had seen a ghost. Or a Goat Boy.

"I'm fine," Jacques said. "They didn't scare me." But his voice trembled as he spoke.

Andrew and Austin were still laughing when Mr. Dingle jogged up, panting and out of breath.

"What's going on?" he asked. "I heard yelling and screaming."

"Just a little Goat Boy fun, Mr. D," said Andrew.

"I thought I gave an explicit order that there was to be no Goat Boy story this year, young man," the camp director snapped.

"I guess I didn't hear you," Austin replied.

"Maybe I was using the bathroom when you gave that order."

Andrew laughed. Mr. Dingle turned red.

Nathaniel was amazed. Sure, Mr. Dingle was a doofus, but he was the adult in charge. These two teenage boys were laughing at him in front of the campers. It was as if Austin and Andrew really ran the camp.

Swell, Nathaniel thought. Just what Camp Spotlight needed, he thought. A couple of bullies running things.

"OK, OK, campers, the evening is over," said Mr. Dingle. "Everyone to their tents. Get a good night's sleep, and tomorrow morning we start on the real purpose of Camp Spotlight — having fun mounting our own musical."

Back in the tent, Brian, Chris and Jacques talked excitedly about the Goat Boy story, and how they had not been afraid for even a second when Andrew came crashing out of the woods.

Nathaniel was quiet, though, puzzling things out in his head. He wondered whether this might have

41

something to do with his parents having been so nervous.

But how could they have known about Andrew and Austin's little trick? They hadn't been to the camp in thirty years.

And why did Austin say the Goat Boy story started thirty years ago, when he had never even met Nathaniel's mom and dad?

If the Goat Boy story was just some prank cooked up by Andrew and Austin, then what *were* his parents worried about?

Was the Goat Boy real, or just a story?

Nathaniel turned these questions over and over in his mind until, finally, he dropped off to sleep.

Chapter Eight

The next day dawned beautiful — clear and sunny, with a light breeze.

Nathaniel woke to hear Jacques chattering away in the sleeping bag next to him, talking to Brian.

Brian hadn't woken up yet, but Jacques was talking to him anyway.

Soon, all four of them were awake. They washed up and ate a pretty disgusting breakfast of runny scrambled eggs and burnt bacon in the mess hall.

"I see why they call it a mess hall," Chris joked.

Then the tent-mates gathered with the other campers in the clearing where the campfire had burned the night before. The memory still lingered in their minds.

Mr. Dingle climbed onto his favorite tree stump and addressed the campers.

"OK, OK, everybody quiet now," he boomed. "We are about to embark on a great and wonderful adventure. In the span of just two weeks, we will rehearse and mount a musical. We'll be doing 'You're a Good Man, Charlie Brown.' First of all, does anyone here *not* want an acting role?"

Two girls and two boys raised their hands.

"Very good, very good," said Mr. Dingle. "You'll be leading our stage crew, then. And you'll get first choice of the backstage jobs since you volunteered. For the rest of you, we have eight primary roles, and ten roles in the back-up chorus. All of the roles except that of Snoopy require a good, strong singing voice and an ability to stay on key. We start auditions now. Follow me!"

He stepped down and walked toward the Camp Spotlight Performance Hall. It was the biggest and nicest building on the camp grounds. It was a solid building, two stories tall and built of red brick.

The campers followed Mr. Dingle, talking

excitedly in small groups. When they entered the Performance Hall, they fell quiet.

It was everything they had dreamed of.

Nearly all of the campers had staged lots of little plays in their garages or basements. They held most rehearsals in their bedrooms.

Now they were in a real, honest-to-goodness theater.

In the auditorium, rows of folding chairs faced the stage. Counselors had placed the wooden benches used around last night's campfire along the back wall.

The stage looked just like a real theater's; in fact, this *was* a real theater. The stage had a heavy red curtain. Lighting fixtures hung overhead, along with microphones. Over on one side of the stage stood a piano.

One of the girl counselors — Nathaniel could see it was the one named Megan who had served him the mystery meat last night for supper — sat at the piano, smiling at them.

She stood up and greeted the campers.

"Welcome to Camp Spotlight," she said. "My

name is Megan, and I'll be playing the piano for 'Charlie Brown.' For auditions, we're going to ask each of you to sing a song.

"Austin is passing out lyric sheets. I'll run through the song several times on the piano so you can get the melody in your heads. Then, one at a time, you'll come up and sing. The best singers will get the primary roles. Any questions?"

The campers were amazed at how fast things were moving, but no one had any questions.

After hearing the song a few times, the campers stepped up onto the stage one by one and sang a little bit. Some were very good, and some were fairly good.

None of them was really bad.

Nathaniel sat on a folding chair. He felt nervous. He'd never sung much before. All of his writing and acting experience involved dramas or comedies, not musicals.

"Nathaniel?" boomed Mr. Dingle.

Nathaniel stepped onto the stage and stood behind the microphone. He took a deep breath and began to sing.

"Thank you!" Mr. Dingle called out.

"But I just got started," Nathaniel protested.

"I know, son, but you were badly off key," Mr. Dingle said. "It's OK. Not everybody has a good singing voice."

Nathaniel was embarrassed. Dweeb man had not allowed him to sing more than a few words! But he wasn't about to show how embarrassed he felt. No way.

He hopped down from the stage and gave a little skip over to his tent-mates.

"Hold it a second, Nathaniel," said Mr. Dingle.

Nathaniel stopped. What now?

"What was that little skip thing you just did?"

"You mean this?" Nathaniel asked, and did it again. It was a variation of the victory dance he did when he scored a touchdown in football, just a funny little shuffling of his feet.

"I like that," said Mr. Dingle. "Nathaniel, you are our Snoopy."

Snoopy? Wasn't that Charlie Brown's *dog*?

"I'm playing the dog?" Nathaniel asked.

"Oh, you're not playing just any dog," Megan spoke up. "Snoopy in some ways is the star of the show. You don't do a whole lot for most of the show, but toward the end the show has a big musical number called 'Suppertime.' You dance around the stage, then run into the audience and pull people out and dance with them.

"If it's done right," Megan said, "you'll bring the house down. I've seen productions of 'Charlie Brown' where Snoopy got the biggest ovation of all."

"OK," Nathaniel said doubtfully.

He was not sure about this at all. He had been cast as a dog.

Was this a lucky break or the worst thing that could happen?

Chapter Nine

It had been a long day.

Nathaniel had wondered aloud about whether being cast as a dog was really the road to future stardom. Several of the counselors had assured him that Snoopy was really a great role, and that he should be honored.

Jacques, Brian and Chris had gotten roles in the chorus, and they were not very happy about that. The role of Charlie Brown had gone to a boy named Reeves from Tent Number Three, whom everyone agreed had an incredible singing voice.

Jillian, the girl with the long red hair, had gotten the role of Lucy. It was the best female part. Nathaniel was happy for her.

Mr. Dingle had declared there would be no stories of any sort at the campfire that night, just a sing-along. He had stayed this time to keep an eye on Andrew and Austin, and had joined heartily into the sing-along.

Unfortunately, Mr. Dingle had a voice as bad as his fashion sense. Nathaniel almost wished he *would* leave, even if it meant that Andrew and Austin would take over again and pull who-knew-what kind of mean prank.

Finally the campfire burned down, and the campers went back to their tents.

Exhausted, Nathaniel climbed into his sleeping bag on top of his cot. His tent-mates did the same.

"That sure was a good story last night," Brian said.

"Yeah," said Jacques. "Goat Boy. Whatever."

Suddenly, Austin poked his head in their tent.

"You guys don't believe in the Goat Boy?" he asked, sounding surprised.

"Yeah, right," said Chris.

"*Sure* we do," said Jacques sarcastically.

"Well, to tell you the truth, I don't know whether the story is real or not," Austin said. "I do know that when I was your age and was a camper here, the counselors told it to us then. Only, they didn't do the jumping-out-of-the-woods part. Me and Andrew made that up just to have some fun with you guys."

"Some fun," muttered Nathaniel.

"Aw, the Goat Boy story is just one of the legends of the camp," Austin said. "Maybe it's true, maybe it isn't. But one time when I was here when I was about twelve, I did cut through the woods. And I found a farm back there that looked like it was abandoned. So maybe it is true."

He stopped and looked at the campers. In spite of themselves, they were paying attention.

"Sleep well, guys," Austin said with a laugh, and pulled his head back out of the tent.

* * *

Exhausted, Nathaniel slept.

Something jolted him awake. He was not sure whether he'd heard something or had just woken up on his own. He glanced out through the open flap of the tent.

It was still the middle of the night.

From a neighboring cot rose the peaceful snore of one of his tent-mates. Nathaniel wasn't sure which. He lay on his bed, staring at the roof of the tent, unable to sleep. He started thinking about Snoopy, and how he would play the part, and whether the audience would laugh when he wanted them to.

Suddenly, he heard a sound. He held his breath and listened.

The sound came from outside his tent. It sounded like scratching, close to the ground. Like an animal digging in the dirt, maybe.

Nathaniel lay very still.

The sound continued. It started getting closer to his tent.

He wondered whether he should wake up his tent-mates. He was tempted to. Maybe one of them could identify the sound, tell him it was just a raccoon scavenging in a garbage can, and he could fall back to sleep.

On the other hand, he didn't want to seem to be a scaredy-cat. There was nothing dangerous about just a little scratching.

Then, he *smelled* it.

Whatever it was smelled like something that had died, been buried, and then dug up. It smelled of dirt, and oldness, and animal. It smelled foul and nasty.

It did *not* smell like a raccoon, Nathaniel thought. Or anything else that would normally prowl around a campground at night.

Then he heard another sound. It seemed to come from a few feet outside the cloth wall of his tent.

"*Meh-hehhhhhh. Meh-hehhhhhh.*"

Nathaniel wondered whether it was the same sound Andrew had made when he hid in the woods during the Goat Boy story.

Then, eerily, terrifyingly close, he heard it again: "*Meh-hehhhhhh. Meh-hehhhhhh.*"

No. It was similar, but not the same.

Whatever was making this sound, it was not Andrew.

Chapter Ten

Nathaniel lay stock still in his sleeping bag. He hardly dared breathe. He was paralyzed with fear.

He heard the noise again: *"Meh-hehhhhhh. Meh-hehhhhhh."*

At least it wasn't getting closer. But it was not getting further away, either. He heard the scratching sound again.

He didn't move. He didn't even blink.

Maybe it was just the counselors playing another trick.

Or maybe it wasn't.

A few minutes passed. Again he heard it: *"Meh-hehhhhhh. Meh-hehhhhhh."*

He sat up and thought about waking his friends. What if they didn't hear anything and said it was his imagination? What if they spread it around camp that he was a big weenie?

And yet he knew — that was the cry of a goat.

A few minutes passed. He did not hear the eerie cry again. The scratching had stopped. He lay back down on his cot and started to relax.

A few more minutes. And a few more. No more sounds. Nothing but the snore of a tent-mate and the wind in the trees.

Finally, he fell back to sleep.

The next morning, Nathaniel awoke before anyone else.

"Hey, guys, rise and shine!" he called.

He was glad it was daylight. Nice bright sunshine would help him forget about last night's noises. Which was exactly what he intended to do.

"Come on, get up you sleepy-heads!" he called.

Grumbling and moaning, Jacques and Brian and Chris began to stretch and squirm around on their cots.

"Who are you, our father?" Chris asked

grumpily.

"Yeah, if Dingle wants to wake us up, that's one thing," Brian said. "You can let us sleep, thanks very much."

"Hey, did you guys hear anything last night?" Nathaniel asked.

They all said no.

"Like what?" asked Jacques.

"Just some noises," Nathaniel said breezily. "They woke me up in the middle of the night."

Jacques started talking as if he were speaking to a baby.

"Oh, and did the widdle noise-ums scare widdle Nathaniel?" Jacques asked. "Did he wet his widdle bed?"

"Yeah, right," Nathaniel said, and leaned over and punched Jacques in the shoulder. Not too hard — but hard enough to show he didn't appreciate being called a baby.

"Maybe it was just your snoring I heard," he said.

He'd been right not to wake these guys up in

the middle of the night, he thought. He never would have heard the end of it.

He remembered something Austin had said when he told the Goat Boy story: Kids can be so cruel.

*   *   *

Breakfast in the mess hall turned out to be yet another lovely dining experience. I must remember to write Mom a letter and have her send more candy bars, Nathaniel thought, because I'm running out.

After breakfast, the campers moved straight to Performance Hall to start rehearsals.

Mr. Dingle had the megaphone, not that he needed one. He shouted at various campers to take certain positions on stage. Megan sat at the piano, smiling and ready for her cue.

Behind the stage, Andrew, Austin, and a counselor named Angela supervised about a dozen campers as they worked on the sets. Enormous backdrops needed to be drawn and painted. The backdrops —

pictures of a baseball diamond, for example, or a class-room — would unfurl behind the actors and set the scene.

Nathaniel looked across the stage and saw Jillian. He stared at her. She looked up and saw him staring. She smiled. He smiled back.

He found his heart was pounding, just as it had when Andrew jumped out of the woods, or when he heard the goat sound in the night. But he wasn't afraid.

Life sure was funny.

"OK, OK! Everybody, on your marks!" Mr. Dingle shouted into the general confusion. "Places, everybody, please. Places, please!"

The campers involved in the first scene went to their assigned positions.

Charlie Brown and Lucy and Linus stood over on the far left side of the stage. Snoopy had to sit on his doghouse on the far right side of the stage. But the doghouse hadn't been built yet, so Nathaniel had to sit on a folding chair. He'd get the doghouse when it was done.

Some kids were still milling around. Mr. Dingle was trying to calm things down so rehearsals could start.

Suddenly Nathaniel heard someone scream, "Look out! Look out!"

It was Megan. She had stood up from her piano bench and was pointing into the air just over Nathaniel's head.

One of the gigantic lighting fixtures was starting to fall. It stood on some metal poles and was about twenty feet high. The light itself was almost as big as a dishwasher and probably weighed several hundred pounds.

But Nathaniel had no time to think about how much it weighed. The light broke loose. In less than a second, it would fall right on top of him.

And it would crush him like a foot crushing a grape.

Chapter Eleven

Nathaniel jumped from his chair and dived forward. He hit the wooden stage with the same splat the mystery meat had made in his plate that first night.

Behind him, he heard a crash.

He looked over his shoulder. He could hardly recognize the chair he'd been sitting in. He saw nothing but pieces of twisted metal.

The enormous stage light had smashed into the chair and practically obliterated it.

If Megan hadn't shouted, Nathaniel would have been killed.

Mr. Dingle and a bunch of campers rushed to where Nathaniel lay on the stage. He was badly shaken, and hitting the stage that hard had knocked the wind out of him. Several arms helped him to his feet.

"Are you all right?"

"My gosh, you could have been killed!"

"What happened?"

It seemed as if everyone was talking to him and asking him questions all at once. He was already dazed, and this made him even more confused.

"Back up everybody," he heard a voice say, "and give the boy some breathing room."

He looked up and it was Angela, the counselor who had been working with the stage crew. She seemed to be the only person there to keep her wits about her.

The campers and staff backed away and started to settle down.

"You need any first aid? Anything broken?" Angela asked Nathaniel.

"I think I'm OK," he said.

This drama stuff can be deadly, he thought.

Mr. Dingle wrung his hands over and over as if he were washing them, but without any soap or water.

"My dear boy! My dear, dear boy," he said over and over. Everyone ignored him.

Angela stood next to Nathaniel, and she seemed calm and in control. That helped Nathaniel calm down, too. He took a deep breath and shook his head.

"I'm all right now," he said. "Thanks."

*   *   *

For the next three days, rehearsals went well.

For the next three nights, the Goat Boy stayed away.

Nathaniel settled into his role as Snoopy. He and Angela worked on some of the dance steps. They were not very complicated. He was supposed to dance free-form, as if he were very happy.

"Suppertime," which was the name of the song, was Snoopy's favorite time of the day — as anybody who's ever owned a dog knows.

Austin and Andrew seemed nicer, or at least not *too* mean. They had given up trying to think up ways to scare the daylights out of the campers.

After the accident with the light, Jillian had

come over and said hello. Nathaniel had become a celebrity because of his brush with death. He was glad she'd said hello. They were never going to be boyfriend and girlfriend, but it was nice to have another friend besides Jacques, Brian and Chris.

Everything went so well that Nathaniel forgot about his parents' nervousness. He forgot about the Goat Boy. He forgot about whatever had made the strange noise and given off the strange stink odor outside his tent in the middle of the night.

Then one night he went to climb into his sleeping bag. As he turned down the top corner, he noticed a note stuck there. He picked it up and read the two brief sentences.

As he read them, his blood seemed to freeze in his veins.

"I'm ready for my Suppertime," the note read. "Will you be my supper?"

It was signed, "Kenny."

Chapter Twelve

Nathaniel just stood there, holding the piece of paper in his hand.

This was a joke. Wasn't it?

"What's that?" asked Chris.

"It's a note from the Goat Boy," said Nathaniel.

"Yeah, right," said Jacques. "Let me see." He reached out and took the paper. "Man, you weren't lying," he said. "It *is* from the Goat Boy."

"If the Goat Boy really exists," said Brian.

"It was probably written by those turkeys Andrew and Austin," Nathaniel said. He was trying to keep calm, trying to not freak out.

But it wasn't easy. It's not every day that an eleven-year-old kid from the suburbs finds himself in the woods without his parents — and threatened with being eaten.

"Yeah, it was probably just them," said Chris.

"Maybe it was, and maybe it wasn't," said Jacques. "They haven't done anything since that first night, around the campfire. They haven't mentioned the Goat Boy again, and they haven't pulled any more pranks. Why, all of a sudden, would they just come and do this?"

"I don't know," said Nathaniel. He remembered the midnight sounds outside the tent, and the haunting cry of the animal that had sounded different from the sound Andrew had made.

Nathaniel decided he had to trust his friends. They seemed spooked by the note, too. Maybe they could look out for each other. Four of them could be stronger and better prepared than just one.

"There's something I haven't told you guys about," he said.

As they gathered around him, he told them about having heard the scratching sounds in the middle of the night, and about the smell and the strange goat-like cry.

When he finished, his three tent-mates sat very quietly. No one made fun of him. No one called him a baby or a scaredy-cat or a weenie.

"Whoo, man," Brian said at last.

"Yeah," agreed Chris.

Jacques, for once, was speechless.

"So the question is, is the Goat Boy for real?" Nathaniel said. "Or is there no such thing as the Goat Boy, and this is just Austin and Andrew having some more fun with us?"

"I don't know," Brian said quietly.

None of them did. But, whatever the answers, it was time for bed.

*   *   *

Nathaniel woke up in the middle of the night.

But he was not awakened by some little sound off in the distance. Instead, he woke up and found himself inside a living nightmare.

Only it was no dream. He was wide awake.

He couldn't move. Not at all. And everything

was totally black!

He felt like he was blind and paralyzed.

Someone had zipped him into his sleeping bag!

His sleeping bag had a zipper that ran all the way around it. While he had slept, someone or something had crept into his tent and quietly pulled the top of his sleeping bag over his head. Then whatever it was had sneakily zipped the zipper all the way around the top.

He was trapped and helpless inside his own sleeping bag.

Then it got worse.

He smelled the odor.

The same sickening, gross smell of dirt and animal and decay.

The smell he had come to think of as coming from the Goat Boy.

Something thudded onto his sleeping bag. Then he felt another thud, which just missed his chest.

Whatever had sealed him inside his sleeping bag was trying to hit him!

Chapter Thirteen

Trapped, terrified and under attack, Nathaniel decided he didn't care a hoot about being thought of as a scaredy-cat. He screamed.

"HELP! HELP!" he yelled. "Somebody help me!"

Then he heard his tent-mates calling for help, too. They must have been sealed into their sleeping bags, as well.

"Help!" Jacques cried out.

"Aaaaah!" was all Chris managed to get out.

The pounding on Nathaniel's sleeping bag ended. He heard footsteps running away.

But he was still trapped.

He yelled again. So did Chris, Brian and Jacques. Their voices formed a chorus of screams. As he took a breath, Nathaniel heard the footsteps returning.

They approached the tent, paused, then came inside.

The Goat Boy was coming back!

He screamed again.

Then he heard the sound of a zipper, and fresh air flooded over him. Desperately, he wriggled to get his head and shoulders out of their prison.

It was Mr. Dingle.

"Mr. Dingle, thank goodness . . . " Nathaniel started to say. But Mr. Dingle had moved to the other side of the tent and was unzipping the other boys' sleeping bags.

All four boys gasped for air.

"What's going on here?" Mr. Dingle asked.

"We don't know," said Nathaniel. "We were all asleep and suddenly we were zipped into our sleeping bags and couldn't get out and someone was pounding on us."

"Is everybody OK? Anybody hurt?" the camp director asked.

The boys said that they were scared but not injured.

"Hmmmm," said Mr. Dingle. "I suspect the

fine hands of a certain pair of counselors. Come with me, boys."

He picked up his heavy flashlight and marched out of the tent. The boys looked at each other, then followed him, in their T-shirts, shorts and bare feet.

Mr. Dingle and the four boys walked through the main clearing and approached two small cottages near Performance Hall. The female counselors lived in one of the cottages, and the male counselors lived in the other.

Mr. Dingle walked up to Austin and Andrew's cottage, and flung the door open.

The cottage was dark. Two beds stood side-by-side in the gloom. And on each bed lay a counselor, fast asleep.

Chapter Fourteen

Mr. Dingle hit the switch, flooding the room with light.

"Up and at 'em, guys!" he shouted.

Austin and Andrew opened their eyes. They blinked several times.

"What's going on?" they asked at the same time.

"What have you two been up to tonight?" Dingle asked.

"Sleeping, man," said Andrew. "Until now, that is."

Dingle waved his arm at Nathaniel and his tent-mates. "You didn't go to these boys' tent?" Dingle boomed.

"Yeah, that's our idea of fun — getting up in the middle of the night and go hang out with 11-year-old kiddies," said Austin.

"I'm a little tired of your sarcasm, young man," said Mr. Dingle.

Austin and Andrew exchanged nervous glances. Usually, they walked right over the Dingle-meister, as they called him behind his back. But, from the looks on their faces, they were wondering if the Dingle-meister had finally grown a spine.

Andrew tried a bluff, anyway.

"Well, we're a little tired, too," he said. "Let me tell you why. We work like dogs all day at this camp and then try to get a little sleep so we can get up and work like dogs again. And now these wee ones come in here accusing us of doing who knows what in their tents."

"Well, since there were no eyewitnesses, there's nothing I can do," Dingle said reluctantly. "But if you step out of line, I'm the guy who's gonna put you right back."

He puffed out his chest, which made his bathrobe gap in the middle. He looked ridiculous.

"Yes, sir!" Andrew and Austin said, and saluted him.

"Come on, boys," Dingle said to Nathaniel and his friends, and they left the cottage.

From behind them as they walked away, Nathaniel thought he heard the sound of laughter.

*   *   *

The next morning, Nathaniel went to see the camp director again.

He had to figure out whether a Goat Boy really existed, or whether everything had just been trickery by Austin and Andrew.

He had to know.

He knocked on Mr. Dingle's office door. The camp director let him in and led him to a couch.

"Still concerned about last night?" he asked.

"Yeah, I guess I am," Nathaniel said.

He paused while he summoned up his courage.

"What can you tell me about the Goat Boy?" he asked finally.

"Oh, the Goat Boy," Dingle said. "Is that what

this is about? Let me tell you what I know."

He sat down behind his desk and pursed his lips.

"I've only been at Camp Spotlight for ten years," he said. "But the camp director before me told me the story. It's a camp tradition for counselors to gather campers around a campfire on the first night, and tell them this silly story about a half-human, half-goat that eats everything.

"I've tried to put a stop to the nonsense, but the tradition seems to be very deeply rooted. The counselors always find a way to get the story in. What worries me, though, is that this year, two of my counselors seem to have taken the Goat Boy stuff to another level. If indeed it was really them who trapped you in your sleeping bags last night."

"What do you mean *if* it was them?" Nathaniel asked. "If it wasn't them, then what was it?"

"Oh, I'm sure it was them," Mr. Dingle said. "Otherwise, it would have had to have been the real Goat Boy!"

He chuckled at his joke.

But Nathaniel did not feel confident enough to joke about this whole situation. It was fine for Dingle to yuk it up. Dingle hadn't nearly been killed by a falling light, or found a threatening note in his bed, or been beaten in the middle of the night — all in the space of one week.

Nathaniel left the camp director's office feeling no better than when he came in.

But he did have an idea.

At first it scared him. But the more he thought about it, the more he knew he had to do it. He could not go on like this.

He had to know. He had to go through the woods, and find the farm.

Only then would he know the truth.

Chapter Fifteen

The next morning was consumed with re-hearsals for "You're a Good Man, Charlie Brown." But Nathaniel's thoughts were consumed with his plan.

At lunch, he told his tent-mates what he intended to do.

"You want to do what?" asked Brian in disbelief.

"I'm going," said Nathaniel. "That's all there is to it. The only question is, are any of you guys going to go with me? Or are you going to weenie out?"

Few eleven-year-old boys want anyone to think they weenied out.

"I'm in," said Jacques, but he didn't sound too sure.

Brian and Chris said they would come, too.

"Good," said Nathaniel. "This afternoon, when we break from rehearsals, we have a couple of hours of free time before dinner. Most of the kids will be swimming or doing other stuff. We can go then and be back before anybody misses us."

"This afternoon?" Jacques repeated nervously.

"Do I smell just a little bit of Oscar Mayer?" Nathaniel asked.

It took Jacques a second to get the joke.

"Hey, I ain't no weenie!" he said.

"OK, then," said Nathaniel. "This afternoon."

*   *   *

When rehearsal ended at four that afternoon, the boys walked casually back to their tent as if nothing in the world was going on.

They changed into long pants in case the woods were full of brambles and stickers.

They looked at each other. Nathaniel felt a little anxious.

More than a little, actually.

What were they about to do? Were they insane? If there really *was* a Goat Boy, did they plan to just walk up to his house?

Then what? Ring the doorbell, and say, "Excuse me please, Mr. Goat Boy, sir, would you please stop creeping around our tent at night and bothering us?"

No, he told himself. They were only going to look, and to find out whatever they could. Before they could think of what to do, they needed to know the truth — whether they were facing some hideous half-human monster or two teenagers with sick senses of humor.

They stepped out of the tent and headed for the woods. At the edge of the forest, they picked up a narrow, winding path.

"How do we know we're going in the right direction?" Brian asked.

"We don't," said Nathaniel. He had somehow become the leader of the group. Maybe it was because the expedition was his idea, or maybe because some kids are just naturally leaders.

Branches hung low over the trail and slapped their faces. They walked carefully in single file, with Nathaniel at the front. They scanned the ground to watch for roots that might trip them. They had to remind themselves to look up now and then so they wouldn't get smacked in the face by a branch.

"Everybody OK?" Nathaniel whispered.

He hadn't planned to whisper, but now that they were actually in the woods — now that they might be near the house — whispering came naturally.

They walked about half an hour. Then the trail just ended.

Ahead of them lay a thick tangle of bushes. It looked as if no human had ever come through this way before.

"Let's keep going," Nathaniel whispered. He parted the brush carefully with his hands, and waded in. The others followed.

They didn't have far to go through the thick foliage, which was good, because they tired quickly. It took only a few minutes of thrashing through the undergrowth.

Then, suddenly, as if by magic, it ended. They looked out onto a barren field. No crop grew here.

The air was still. They heard no birds chirping, nor any insects humming. Just the breathing of four boys at the edge of a field.

Nathaniel pointed. About half a mile away stood a farmhouse.

<u>Chapter Sixteen</u>

"This is it, guys," Nathaniel whispered.

"It sure is," Jacques said.

"Anybody coming with me?" Nathaniel asked.

"I'll stand look-out," Chris said.

"Me, too," said Brian.

"Me, too," said Jacques.

Nathaniel knew they were afraid. He knew because he was, too. But this wasn't a time for name-calling. This was a time for action. He hadn't come all this way to turn around and go back to camp.

"Holler if you see anything," he said.

Slowly, he began to walk across the field. Each step carried him closer to the farmhouse. What had looked so small a few minutes ago loomed larger and larger the closer he got.

The dirt field changed over to grass. Nathaniel realized he had crossed into the farmer's yard.

Now he stood right next to the house. He walked up to a window. His legs trembled.

He looked in. There were no lights on, so it was a little hard to see. But the window looked in on the kitchen.

He saw the kitchen table. There were dishes on it. There was food on it.

The farmhouse was not abandoned.

Then he heard the sound of Chris's voice, shouting in panic.

"Run, Nathaniel, run!" Chris yelled.

But before he could run, Nathaniel felt a hand grip his shoulder.

Chapter Seventeen

"Just what the heck do you think you're doing?" said a voice.

Nathaniel tried to turn, but the hand stayed on his shoulder. The grip was tight, like a vise. His shoulder hurt.

He turned his head and found himself looking into a plaid shirt.

He looked up and saw the weathered face of an old man. The man's hair was white, long and scraggly. It looked as if it hadn't been combed in months. White stubble dotted the man's chin. He hadn't shaved in at least a week.

"I asked you a question, you little trespasser," the man hissed. "What are you doing spying on me?"

Nathaniel was breathing so hard from the shock that he could barely get his words out.

"I'm sorry, sir. I'm really really sorry." His voice sounded squeaky.

How had he gotten himself into this mess?

He glanced back to the thicket of brush where his three tent-mates had last been. He saw no sign of them.

Had they run away? Were they hiding? One thing was certain — they sure weren't trying to rescue him.

And why should they? They weren't the ones who had gotten caught. They weren't the ones who had come up with the dumbest idea in history.

"You didn't answer my question," the farmer snarled. "I bet you're sorry. Sorry you got caught. Now tell me what you're doing here."

Nathaniel's mind raced. Should he tell the truth, and say he was looking for the Goat Boy? What if the Goat Boy was real, and this old man was his father? Or what if the Goat Boy was not real, and this guy decided he was insane.

"I don't know, sir," was Nathaniel's feeble reply.

The man's hand was amazingly strong, considering how old he was. Nathaniel couldn't tell if he was sixty, seventy, eighty or ninety. It can be hard to tell with people that old. He just knew that the iron grip digging into his shoulder really hurt.

"You don't *know*?" the farmer said, mocking him. "You're peeping in my kitchen window and you don't *know* why you're doing it?"

"Can I please go now, sir?" Nathaniel pleaded.

"No," snapped the farmer. "You cannot."

Chapter Eighteen

"You ain't going nowhere until you tell me what's going on," the old man said. "Are you one of those snot-nosed little punks from that Camp Spotlight?"

Nathaniel nodded.

"And I'll bet you came here because you heard a story, didn't you?" the farmer asked.

Nathaniel nodded again. What else could he do? Obviously, the farmer had figured out what was what.

"So you're in search of the Goat Boy, huh?" the old man said. "Well, well. A brave little camper decided to come snooping around. Didn't have enough to do prancing around on the stage with a bunch of rich kids. Had to kick up a little extra excitement for himself."

He leaned his face down into Nathaniel's. His breath smelled like old chewing tobacco.

"Well, is *this* exciting enough for you?" He shook Nathaniel and laughed a nasty little laugh.

"Please, sir," Nathaniel pleaded. "I'll never bother you again. Please let me go."

"Tell you what, son," the old man said. "If you're so interested in the Goat Boy, why don't I show you around the place. Maybe you'll see that there's just me living here all by myself."

The farmer grinned, exposing brown, tobacco-stained teeth.

"Or maybe we'll go inside and meet the Goat Boy," he said. "And maybe he'll be *hungry*." He laughed again.

"Or," he continued, "I could just call the police and have you arrested for trespassing. Quite a few nice little options I've got, I'd say."

Nathaniel shivered. This situation was becoming worse every second.

Where were his friends? Were they already back at camp? Maybe they were getting someone to come save him. Maybe they were devising a plan to help him escape. Maybe they were huddled in the bushes right now, scared to death and trying to figure out what to do.

"Come along, son," said the farmer. "Let's have a little tour of the old farm. You can call me Mr. McDonald. That's not my real name, but I like the sound of it."

He began to sing in a croaky, off-key voice: "Old McDonald had a farm, E-I-E-I-O. And on this farm he had some goats. E-I-E-I-O.

"Shall we go check out the goats?" he asked.

Holding Nathaniel firmly by the shoulder, the old man walked him around the side of the house. About a hundred yards from the house, Nathaniel saw a fenced-in area with about thirty goats in it.

Some munched on hay; others slept. They didn't seem terribly threatening.

"There's my goats," the farmer said. "Any of them look half-human to you?"

Nathaniel shook his head. He still found it hard to talk.

"You may be wondering how I know about the Goat Boy story," the old man said.

Actually, it had not occurred to Nathaniel to wonder that at all, but the farmer told him anyway.

"You think I can live so close to that dang Camp Spotlight for thirty years and not hear about the Goat Boy?" the farmer spat. "You think you're the first kid who ever got the idea to cut through the woods and check out this place?"

Nathaniel shook his head again. It seemed like the nightmare would never end.

And it wouldn't. Not for a while.

Chapter Nineteen

The farmer guided Nathaniel up some rickety steps and across the front porch of the farm house.

The house looked as if it had been painted yellow years ago, but the sun had faded most of the color away. The paint that remained had peeled and chipped. Now the house looked mottled, with streaks of yellow mingling with bits of gray and brown.

They went in the front door. Everything smelled old and unused.

"This here's my entry way," the farmer said, gesturing with one hand while the other maintained its grip on Nathaniel's shoulder. "Over there's my living room, although I don't do a whole lot of living in there anymore."

He chuckled as if he had made a joke.

"Through there's the kitchen, which I guess

you've already seen," he said. "Upstairs there are two bedrooms and a bathroom."

He smiled, showing his brown teeth again. "The Goat Boy," he said, "lives in the basement."

Nathaniel looked at the old man. Was he kidding?

"That's a joke, ya little snoop," the farmer spat. "There is no Goat Boy. Now get out of here before I call the cops."

He released Nathaniel's shoulder.

Nathaniel did not need to be told twice. Over his shoulder he heard the man say, "And let that be a lesson to you," but he was already running through the house, down the porch steps, and toward the woods.

He ran faster than he'd ever made any fast break in basketball, and faster than any football play had ever required of him.

It had taken him ten minutes to walk from the woods to the farmhouse. He made it back in about two.

He saw his friends where he had left them, where the woods met the field. They ran, too, crashing through the tangled brush, back toward camp, which suddenly seemed like the safest place in the universe.

Nathaniel flailed his way through the brush. A few hundred yards up the trail, he caught up to his friends, doubled over breathing hard.

"What happened?" they all asked at once.

"Later," was all Nathaniel could manage as he gasped for air. "Just run!"

*   *   *

They stood panting in their tent, safe at last. When he caught his breath, Nathaniel told them the entire story.

His friends listened with their mouths hanging open.

This had not been a prank. This was real! That crazy old guy really could have hurt Nathaniel.

Supper in the mess hall that night was uneventful — if you call it uneventful when the cook forgets to cook the noodles and bakes them into the lasagna hard, the way they come in the package.

"Well, you can always count on the food here," cracked Jacques. "The quality never varies."

That night was uneventful, too. And the next day. And the next.

The end of camp was approaching. Only one more day until their parents would come to see the one and only Camp Spotlight performance of "You're a Good Man, Charlie Brown."

Nathaniel was so at ease with his big "Suppertime" dance he could do it in his sleep. The stage crew had finished building his doghouse, and a dandy doghouse it was. They had his name right above the door: "Snoopy."

The other kids had learned their lines and mastered their songs. No more lights had fallen. Even Andrew and Austin had toned it down, and weren't being very mean to the campers.

"Excellent! Most excellent!" Mr. Dingle proclaimed at the final rehearsal.

He was wearing a maroon cardigan sweater and lime green shorts. He clapped his hands with glee at what he had achieved as a director in two short weeks.

"After dinner tonight, we're not going to have a campfire," he said. "I know it's your last night, but we have to get a good night's sleep so everyone is rested for the show tomorrow. Parents arrive about noon. Showtime is two p.m."

So, for the final night, Nathaniel and his friends crawled into their sleeping bags in Tent Number Five.

It would be a night he would never forget.

Chapter Twenty

"E-e-e-e-e-e-e-e-e-e!"

The scream seemed to drill right into Nathaniel's brain. He jumped up out of his sleeping bag.

He heard the scream again. It was high-pitched and piercing. It sounded like a girl.

It sounded like Jillian.

He raced from the tent. He was vaguely aware of his tent-mates running behind him. When he reached the campfire clearing, he looked up and saw Jillian racing toward him from the direction of the girls' bathroom.

She was still screaming.

Other campers emptied out of their tents. Mr. Dingle trotted up. It seemed as if the entire camp met in the middle of the clearing.

There were no lights, and there had been no

campfire. The darkness amplified the fear and confusion everyone felt.

Everyone shouted at Jillian — Nathaniel, Mr. Dingle, and a dozen other campers — asking what the matter was.

"The Goat Boy!" Jillian shouted. "The Goat Boy! I saw him!"

Several campers snorted. A few laughed. Most of them had not endured the experiences Nathaniel had.

"Calm down, calm down," said Mr. Dingle, "and try to tell us what happened."

"I got up to go to the bathroom," Jillian said.

There were no bathrooms in the tents, of course. The girls used a bathroom with toilets, showers and sinks at one end of a big, cinderblock building. The boys had the same arrangement at the other end.

"As I was washing my hands, I looked out through one of the windows. This goat head stared right back at me! He had red eyes, and fangs with blood on them! It was horrible!"

"There, there," said Mr. Dingle. "Are you sure

it wasn't a dream, honey?"

Jillian's voice became icy.

"Yes, I'm sure it wasn't a dream. I don't usually dream in the bathroom. I tend to do my dreaming in my tent. And I didn't run here from my tent, I ran here from the bathroom."

"Hmmmm," was all Mr. Dingle had to say to that.

Nathaniel wanted to tell Jillian that he thought the whole Goat Boy business was just a trick by the counselors, and that he had just been through the farmhouse today. And that, while the farmer was as mean as they came, the house had no Goat Boy in it.

But, of course, he couldn't. That would be admitting to everyone that he had trespassed at the farmhouse and been busted by the old farmer. It would be too embarrassing.

So he kept quiet.

"It was the Goat Boy!" Jillian kept repeating. "It really was. I saw his face. He was looking at me!"

Mr. Dingle didn't seem to know what to do.

"OK, OK everybody," he said. "Nothing's

really going on here. Let's all go back to our tents. Jillian, Vanessa, Mary, Rebecca, I'll walk you all back to your tent to make sure everything's OK."

Nathaniel decided the excitement was over. He walked slowly back to his tent. The other campers dispersed also, muttering quietly as they walked back to the different parts of the camp.

Thunder rumbled in the distance.

Then, over the hum of voices, Nathaniel heard a loud, booming shout.

"What the heck is going on here? When I find out who . . . "

It was Mr. Dingle, yelling his head off.

"Someone is going to be held responsible! When I get to the bottom of this . . . "

Nathaniel ran to Mr. Dingle's cabin. He looked in the open door and saw Mr. Dingle standing in the middle of his cabin, still yelling.

The cabin had been practically destroyed. Someone or something had tossed things from one side of the room to another. Mr. Dingle was normally a very neat person, but now the whole room was chaos. Pictures tilted on the walls, his clothes had been thrown all over the floor, lamps had been knocked over. Even his bed covers were messed up.

In the center of the bed lay one of Mr. Dingle's sandals. Even from the doorway, Nathaniel saw something that made his his heart stop.

The sandal was covered with teeth marks. It had been badly chewed.

Chapter Twenty-One

The lightning lit up the campgrounds as if it were noon. The roaring boom of thunder shook the tents of the campers.

Nathaniel sat bolt upright in his cot.

The night's excitement had finally subsided. Mr. Dingle had shooed the campers away from his cabin. They had returned to their own tents. Everyone had, at last, fallen asleep.

Nathaniel had never been afraid of thunderstorms. But this one was a doozy, parked right over the camp, shooting down lightning and rattling the tents with thunder.

Amanda was the one afraid of thunderstorms. She wouldn't have liked this one at all, Nathaniel thought.

That's funny, he thought. I've been so busy rehearsing for "Charlie Brown" and worrying about the Goat Boy that I haven't thought of Amanda in two weeks. It will actually be good to see her tomorrow.

He shook the sleeping bag off his shoulders to free his arms. He listened to the rain pelting the tent. The tent was water-proof, thank goodness. He was as dry as if he had been sleeping in an oven.

But then he looked at the end of the tent closest to his feet.

The tent flaps were tied open. If the wind shifted, buckets of rain would blow inside the tent and soak them all.

He thought maybe he should get up and tie the flaps closed. He pulled his feet out of his sleeping bag and swung them over the edge of the cot. They hit the wood-plank floor of the tent.

Another bolt of lightning even more powerful than the first crackled across the sky. It lit up everything, like a huge flash bulb in the night.

It lit up the opening of the tent flap.

It lit up the figure standing there. The figure wearing a long dark coat.

The figure with the head of a goat.

Nathaniel froze, unsure if the Goat Boy had seen him.

He smelled the awful, decayed odor.

The Goat Boy was far more hideous than anything he could imagine. He had yellow, pointed fangs, smeared with something red. Something that looked a lot like blood.

His eyes were red, too. And evil-looking.

Nathaniel clutched his sleeping bag to his chest. He was face-to-face with the Goat Boy.

Chapter Twenty-Two

Nathaniel glanced wildly at his tent-mates. They were sound asleep. The thunder had not disturbed them.

He looked toward the back of the tent. The flaps there had been tied closed. He could not escape out the back.

Nathaniel and the monster stared at each other for about a second. It was the longest second of Nathaniel's life.

If he stayed where he was, he didn't stand a chance.

His only hope was the little bit of space between the tent flap and the monster's black coat. If he could squeeze through that opening, maybe he could outrace the creature to Mr. Dingle's room.

That would mean running straight at the Goat

Boy. That was insanity!

But it was the only way. He had to do it.

Two more seconds had ticked by.

The Goat Boy took a step into the tent, right towards Nathaniel.

He had no more time for thinking. It was time for action.

He jumped from his cot and was running when he hit the floor.

The creature paused.

Nathaniel sprinted for the opening. But it wasn't big enough. He would not be able to squeeze through.

The creature lifted its arms toward Nathaniel.

He couldn't stop now. He had to keep going.

Running at top speed, he hit the Goat Boy on the side. The monster was solidly built. Pain tore through Nathaniel's body.

But the Goat Boy staggered to one side, surprised and knocked off balance by Nathaniel's charge.

Nathaniel burst through the opening.

As he looked back, he saw the strangest thing he had seen so far.

The creature's head fell off!

Chapter Twenty-Three

"Hey!" the Goat Boy yelled.

Nathaniel stopped. He knew that voice! Slowly, he turned to look.

"Andrew?" he said.

"If you ruined this head, I'm gonna kill you, you little punk," Andrew spat out.

Chris stuck his head out of the tent.

"What's going on?" he asked.

The coat had been pulled up around Andrew's head, with the head of a goat on top of that. The effect had been terrifying.

Now, Andrew let the coat fall back around his shoulders.

Jacques and Brian now appeared at the front of the tent.

Slowly, Nathaniel walked back to face Andrew. The two of them stood facing each other, their eyes locked. Neither noticed the rain that fell in sheets and soaked them both.

Andrew picked up the head where it had fallen in the dirt.

"Do you have any idea how much trouble it was to make this?" he demanded.

Austin came running up, drenched from the rain.

"Did it work?" he asked Andrew. Then he saw Andrew holding the goat's head, and the four campers standing there.

"Oh," he said.

Nathaniel reached out and snatched the goat's head from Andrew. He cradled it under his arm like a football and took off in a sprint for Mr. Dingle's room.

"Hey! Come back you little twerp!" Austin yelled.

Andrew and Austin raced after Nathaniel.

Chris, Brian and Jacques followed, running like mad through the pouring rain. Lightning flashed and thunder bellowed.

Nathaniel ran to Mr. Dingle's door and started pounding. The camp director opened the door just as Austin and Andrew ran up, skidding and sliding on the muddy ground.

From the looks on their faces, the counselors realized now that chasing Nathaniel there had not been a good idea.

"What's the meaning of this?" Mr. Dingle asked.

Nathaniel held the goat's head out in front of him. Mr. Dingle looked at the head, then at Austin and Andrew, who stood behind Nathaniel.

"Oooh, busted!" Jacques whooped. Austin shot him a nasty look.

Mr. Dingle ordered all the boys into his room and made them sit down. He listened to Nathaniel's story first. Then he asked Andrew and Austin about the goat's head.

Austin said his dad was a taxidermist — a person who stuffs dead animals so they can be displayed. Usually, a hunter wants to stuff the head of a deer he has shot, or a fisherman may want to stuff an exceptionally large fish he has landed. Properly stuffed, the animals can be mounted and hung on a wall as a trophy.

Last year, a man had brought a goat's head in to the taxidermy shop and asked Austin's dad to stuff and preserve it. He said he was playing a joke on a hunter friend who always bragged about his collection of deer's heads. But the man never came back to pick up the goat's head.

The head wound up sitting in a storeroom in the back of the shop.

Before coming to camp this summer, Austin said, he had stolen the goat's head. Then he and Andrew had cooked up the whole series of stunts, just to scare the campers.

They had written the note, theoretically signed by Kenny, and left it on Nathaniel's bed. They had zipped the boys in Tent Number Five into their sleeping bags, wanting only to scare them, not to hurt them.

They had seen Jillian go into the bathroom and had held the goat head up to the window to frighten her.

"Boys, that really stinks," Mr. Dingle boomed. "Really stinks."

"We know. We're sorry," Austin said.

"No, I mean that goat's head really stinks. Is it starting to go bad?"

"Yeah, I guess maybe my dad didn't finish the job," Austin said. "Properly stuffed animals don't stink at all. But this smells really awful."

Now Nathaniel knew why he had smelled such a terrible odor during the Goat Boy attacks.

He looked at the head again. The fangs were glued in, and the blood was red paint. They had taken fake rubies and put them in the eyes to make them glow red.

"The hardest thing for me to believe," Mr. Dingle boomed, "is that you two would break into my quarters and do whatever it was you did to make one of my shoes appear chewed up. I consider that vandalism. That was my favorite pair of sandals."

Austin looked at Andrew.

Andrew looked at Austin.

"Beg your pardon, sir?" Andrew said.

"You know what I'm talking about," Mr. Dingle fired back.

"Honestly, sir, we didn't chew your shoes," Austin said.

"Right, right," said Dingle. "Do you think I was born yesterday?"

Austin and Andrew looked at each other, puzzled.

"I'll deal with you fellows tomorrow when your parents come to pick you up," Mr. Dingle said. "I hope by then you're ready to confess to damaging my shoe. You should at least have the maturity to own up to what you've done."

For once, Austin and Andrew didn't have anything to say.

"Let's get some sleep," the camp director said. "We've still got a play to do tomorrow."

Chapter Twenty-Four

Camp Spotlight's Performance Hall was packed.

Every chair held a proud parent, or a brother or sister. Some grandparents were sprinkled throughout the crowd, too. About half the dads had camcorders perched on their shoulders. They knelt in the aisles and set up tripods and jockeyed for the best camera positions.

Mr. Dingle strode onto the stage. The crowd fell silent, except for the occasional chatter of a younger child.

"Ladies and gentlemen," Mr. Dingle boomed, "Camp Spotlight is proud to present 'You're a Good Man, Charlie Brown!'"

He marched off. The mothers and fathers and brothers and sisters waited in silence. The only sound was the shuffling of programs.

As the curtain rose, Nathaniel was perched on top of his doghouse. He was dressed in white jeans and a white turtleneck, and had black construction-paper spots glued to his clothes. A fake rubber dog's nose was strapped over his own. Long cloth ears flopped down the sides of his face.

When it came time for his big number, "Suppertime," Nathaniel's heart was beating as hard as it had when he ran from the old farmer, or when he had seen the Goat Boy starting to come into his tent.

He jumped down from the doghouse and went into his little shuffle step. Megan pounded away on the piano.

Nathaniel ran out into the audience. He pulled someone's mom up out of her seat, grabbed both her hands, and swung her around. The woman grinned and went along with it. The audience laughed and began clapping in rhythm.

He ran from one person to the next, skipping and dancing. This was great!

His sister, Amanda, was sitting on the end of a

row. Nathaniel danced over to her and swept her out of her seat. She giggled with glee.

Then he ran back on stage and — in one last feat of bravery — danced over to Jillian. She grinned when she saw him coming, and reached her hands out to him.

He took her hands and swung her around. He had never been happier in his entire life.

As he jumped back on top of his doghouse, the audience leaped to its feet and gave him a standing ovation.

When the play was over, and the cast came out one by one for final bows, Nathaniel got the most applause of anyone. Even Reeves, the boy who had played Charlie Brown, got less applause than Nathaniel.

*   *   *

The family minivan was back on the road, heading away from Camp Spotlight.

Nathaniel had said his good-byes to Megan

and Angela, to Jacques, Brian and Chris, and to Jillian.

He had seen Mr. Dingle talking to Andrew and Austin's parents. Both fathers had their arms crossed over their chests and looked sternly at their two sons. They were in for it now, Nathaniel thought, and they deserved it.

Nathaniel did not say good-bye to them.

As the van rolled along, Nathaniel told his parents the story of the Goat Boy, starting with the campfire, the note, and being zipped into his sleeping bag.

He went ahead and told them about going to the farmhouse, even though he knew they would be mad. He told them about the final night, and the appearance of the Goat Boy in the moonlight.

His parents were very quiet. So was Amanda, who had never heard such a strange story before.

Finally his mother spoke.

"It's worse than we imagined," she said to Nathaniel's father.

"We're sorry that all happened to you, son," his father said.

"Is that what you guys were nervous about before I came to camp?" Nathaniel asked.

"How did you know we were nervous?" his mother asked.

Nathaniel told them about the conversation he had overheard.

"Then I guess we'll explain everything," his father said. "I think we owe it to you."

Chapter Twenty-Five

"As we told you," Nathaniel's father said as he drove, "your mother and I went to Camp Spotlight thirty years ago. That's where we first met."

He looked over his shoulder and eased the van onto the highway.

"That year at camp, something horrible happened," he said. "A boy named Kenny, who lived on a farm on the other side of the woods, had been hanging around the camp. Some of the kids had made fun of him, and called him the Goat Boy, because it was his job to tend the goats. One night a tent caught fire for no apparent reason. Nobody was hurt. Everybody assumed that Kenny did it, but no one could prove anything."

"Was there a boy in the tent who's last name was Muldaur?" asked Nathaniel.

"Well, it's been a long time, but I think there was. His father was a stage magician, I think," Nathaniel's dad said.

Nathaniel started to get a very creepy feeling. He felt the hair on the back of his neck start to stand up.

He told his father the part of the story about Muldaur the Magnificent, and how he could work real magic.

"Oh, come on, honey," said his mother. "Surely you know there's no such thing as magic."

"Seriously, Nathaniel," said his father, "everybody went home after it was all over, and I'm sure Kenny went back to tending his goats. You can't cast a spell that turns someone into a half-goat, half-human thing."

Nathaniel's mother took up the tale.

"So when we went back to the camp the next year, on the first night they had a bonfire," she said. "One of the counselors, trying to frighten the new kids, told the story about Kenny burning down the tent. But there wasn't anything in the story about

119

Kenny being turned into a Goat Boy.

"Then a few years later I returned to Camp Spotlight to work as a counselor," she went on. "The legend of Kenny had grown and become more complicated. Every time the counselors told the story, it got weirder. Somewhere in there, the bit about the half-human, half-goat monster was added.

"So when you wanted to go to Camp Spotlight, we called Mr. Dingle and asked if the counselors were still scaring the newcomers with the Goat Boy story. We didn't want you to be frightened."

"Mom, Dad," Nathaniel said, with irritation in his voice. "I'm eleven years old! Come on. I can take a story."

"Well, that's what we decided," his mom said. "Mr. Dingle said he was trying to put an end to the Goat Boy story, but the legend refused to die."

"Of course," his father added, "Mr. Dingle didn't have any idea that Austin and Andrew were going to take it to such a new level, with the goat's head, and all the rest of it. We couldn't predict that either."

"And what about the farmhouse?" Nathaniel asked. "I know that was real."

"Sure it was," said his father. "But it's just a farmhouse. Some mean old farmer lives there all alone. Nothing supernatural about that."

Nathaniel thought about it. It made sense. That's how legends work, he had learned in school. Sometimes you start with a grain of truth, and as the story gets told and re-told, it's built into something much bigger than it originally was.

He thought about his two weeks at Camp Spotlight. What a great time!

Maybe in a few years he'd go back as a counselor. Maybe he'd be the one to tell the story of the Goat Boy.

But there were things he did not know, things no one knew. Such as who, or what, had really chewed Mr. Dingle's sandal.

Chapter Twenty-Six

Camp Spotlight was deserted.

Summer was over. The campers had returned to their cities and suburbs and were preparing to go back to school. The counselors had returned to their high schools.

Mr. Dingle had returned to his job as a community theater director in a small town in the southern part of the state. He had forgotten all about the silliness over the Goat Boy. He had forgotten about the chewed sandal on his bed.

The tents had been taken down and stored in Performance Hall, which was padlocked. They'd be brought out next summer for another group of campers.

All was quiet. A soft breeze blew.

From deep in the woods, though no one was

there to hear it, there came a rustling sound. Then a shuffling and a scratching.

An unpleasant odor floated on the breeze.

In a tree, a flock of birds suddenly cried out and took off, flapping their wings, in one huge group. Their calls contained a hint of fear.

At the farmhouse, the old man walked down the flight of stairs that led to the basement. He held tight to the hand rail, just as he had held tight to Nathaniel's shoulder.

He took out a key and opened a padlock on the basement door. He pushed the door open, and the stench hit him like a punch in the face.

He looked around the basement. It was empty. In a corner, he saw some scraps of leather that looked as if they might have come from someone's shoe, or perhaps a sandal.

"Oh, no," the old man said quietly to himself. "He always manages to get out."

The Goat Boy was on the loose. Again.

ACTIVITY

& PROJECT

BOOKS

Handy Size

Big Value

and always in

Big Demand

An exciting range of project/ability books for inquisitive young minds

Small enough for the pocket ...

Big enough to expand the mind ...

At pocket-money prices

68 pages

£1.00 each including postage and packing

ISBN Prefix - 0 7105 0 Bar Code Prefix - 9 780710 50			No. of Copies Required
ISBN 965 0	Bar Code 9659	Making Musical Instruments	
ISBN 966 9	Bar Code 9666	Conjuring	
ISBN 967 7	Bar Code 9673	Fossil Hunting	
ISBN 968 5	Bar Code 9680	Being An Inventor	
ISBN 969 3	Bar Code 9697	First Aid	
ISBN 970 7	Bar Code 9703	Mapping The Night Sky	
ISBN 971 5	Bar Code 9710	Ponds and Aquariums	
ISBN 972 3	Bar Code 9727	Your Dog	
ISBN 973 1	Bar Code 9734	Your Cat	
ISBN 974 X	Bar Code 9741	Small Pets	
ISBN 975 8	Bar Code 9758	Collecting	
ISBN 976 6	Bar Code 9765	Painting in Watercolour	
ISBN 977 4	Bar Code 9772	Tracing Your Family Tree	
ISBN 978 2	Bar Code 9789	The Weather	
ISBN 979 0	Bar Code 9796	Drawing	
ISBN 980 4	Bar Code 9802	Stamp Collecting	
ISBN 981 2	Bar Code 9819	Learning to Play a Guitar	
ISBN 982 0	Bar Code 9826	Learning to Ride	
ISBN 983 9	Bar Code 9833	Keeping Fit	
ISBN 984 7	Bar Code 9840	Pictures Without Brushes	
ISBN 985 5	Bar Code 9857	Toffee and Sweet Making	
ISBN 986 3	Bar Code 9864	Making Working Models	
ISBN 987 1	Bar Code 9871	Learning to Swim	
ISBN 988 X	Bar Code 9888	Playing Tennis	
ISBN 989 8	Bar Code 9895	Sculpting in Paper	
ISBN 990 1	Bar Code 9901	Cooking	
ISBN 991 X	Bar Code 9918	Secret Codes	
ISBN 992 8	Bar Code 9925	Drawing Figures in Action	
ISBN 993 6	Bar Code 9932	Making Your Own Costumes	
ISBN 994 4	Bar Code 9949	Modelling and Sculpting	

To order, complete the coupon and send to:-

Children's Leisure Products Ltd
Industrial Estate
Pinfold Lane
Bridlington
East Yorkshire
YO16 6BT

Please send the titles listed above to:

Name ....

Address...

....

.... Post Code ....

Cheque/P. Order enclosed   £...................

This offer applicable to the United Kingdom only.